KU-433-437

The Pug who wanted to be a Pumpkin

WITHDRAWN

2 3 JUL 2024

TULLAMORE

Class:
Acc:
Inv:

With special thanks to Anne Marie Ryan.
Illustrations by Nina Jones and Artful Doodlers.

 ORCHARD BOOKS

First published in Great Britain in 2020 by The Watts Publishing Group

1 3 5 7 9 10 8 6 4 2

Text copyright © Orchard Books, 2020
Illustrations copyright © Orchard Books, 2020

The moral rights of the author and illustrator have been asserted.

All characters and events in this publication, other than those clearly in the public domain, are fictitious and any resemblance to real persons, living or dead, is purely coincidental.

All rights reserved.
No part of this publication may be reproduced, stored in a retrieval system, or transmitted, in any form or by any means, without the prior permission in writing of the publisher, nor be otherwise circulated in any form of binding or cover other than that in which it is published and without a similar condition including this condition being imposed on the subsequent purchaser.

A CIP catalogue record for this book
is available from the British Library.

ISBN 978 1 40836 092 7

Printed and bound in Great Britain by Clays Ltd, Elcograf S.p.A
The paper and board used in this book are made from wood from responsible sources.

MIX
Paper from
responsible sources
FSC
www.fsc.org
FSC® C104740

Orchard Books
An imprint of
Hachette Children's Group
Part of The Watts Publishing Group Limited
Carmelite House
50 Victoria Embankment
London EC4Y 0DZ

An Hachette UK Company
www.hachette.co.uk
www.hachettechildrens.co.uk

The Pug who wanted to be a Pumpkin

Bella Swift

Contents

Contents

Chapter One

A big, scary monster stared at Peggy the pug with wild yellow eyes. It roared loudly, showing its sharp teeth. Just as it was about to gobble her up, Peggy woke from her nap with a start.

Phew! thought Peggy. *It was just a dream.* But then she opened her eyes and jumped up in fright. Something scary was coming straight down the hallway towards her. It wasn't a monster, but it was almost as bad – the vacuum cleaner!

"Sorry, Pegs," called Dad, over the noise of the hoover. "I know you hate this thing, but it's Saturday."

Every Saturday afternoon, Peggy's family did chores. Fleeing from the vacuum cleaner, Peggy ran into the living room. Chloe was cleaning the windows while her older brother, Finn, dusted. Ruby, the youngest, was tidying her toys away.

"I'll help too!" said Peggy, picking up a teddy with her teeth and dropping it into a basket. Of course, to the humans it just sounded like barking.

Mum came into the living room and peeled off a pair of yellow rubber gloves. "The kitchen's done. How are you lot getting on in here?"

"Nearly done," said Chloe.

Peggy retrieved a train from under the sofa and dropped it on Ruby's lap. Ruby patted her on the head and giggled. "Peggy's helping too."

"Can me and my friends make pizzas tonight?" Chloe asked as she squirted spray on the windows and cleaned it off with a paper towel.

Mmm, pizza. Just thinking about it

made Peggy drool in anticipation.

"Of course," Mum said.

"And can we make popcorn and watch a scary movie?" asked Chloe. "*Pleeeeease* – it's almost Halloween."

"Yes," said Mum, laughing. "That's all fine."

"Who's sleeping over tonight?" asked Finn, running the duster over the shelves.

"Ellie and Hannah," said Chloe. "We're going to sleep in the lounge. With Peggy, of course."

"Yay!" barked Peggy. She and Chloe had been best friends ever since Chloe's family had adopted Peggy from an animal shelter. Peggy loved everyone in her family, but she and Chloe had always shared a special bond.

"Can we stay up really, really late?" Chloe asked.

"As long as you don't keep the rest of us up," replied Mum.

"Me too," begged Ruby, jumping up and down. "I want to stay up late, too!"

"No way," said Chloe. "You're only in Reception. You're too little for a sleepover party."

"You can stay up a *bit* later than usual, Rubes," said Mum, "but this is Chloe's sleepover."

"Not fair," Ruby said, pouting.

"You'll have your own sleepovers when you're older," Mum promised her.

"You aren't allowed to bother us

either," Chloe told her big brother.

"Don't worry," Finn said, flicking her with the duster. "I don't want to hang out with you and your stupid friends, anyway."

"Good," retorted Chloe, sticking her tongue out at him. "Because you're not invited!"

Peggy couldn't wait for Chloe's friends to arrive. She ran over to the window and jumped up, resting her front paws on the sill. Pressing her flat, black nose against the glass, she looked out at the front garden. The trees were ablaze with red, gold and brown leaves, but there was no sign of Chloe's friends on the path.

"Peggy," sighed Chloe. "I just cleaned that!" She squirted cleaning spray on the window again and wiped away the smudge Peggy's nose had left on the glass. "I want to get it done quickly so I can get ready for my sleepover."

"It's safe to come out, Peggy," said Dad, poking his head round the door. "I've finished hoovering. Anything else need doing?"

"Nope," said Mum. "That's everything. Great job, everyone."

"Come on, Peggy," said Chloe. "We need to plan for tonight!"

Peggy hurried after Chloe, climbing the stairs as fast as her short little legs could go. Sitting cross-legged on her bed, Chloe took out a sparkly notebook with a unicorn on the cover and began to make a list.

"Pizza ... pampering ... popcorn," said Chloe as she wrote.

Peggy thought it all sounded fun – especially the pizza and popcorn! She let out an enthusiastic yip.

"*Hmm* ... Am I forgetting anything?"

Chloe wondered out loud.

Peggy chewed on the corner of Chloe's pillow thoughtfully.

"Oh, that reminds me!" Chloe said, tugging the pillow out of Peggy's mouth. "We need to have a pillow fight, too!" She quickly added "pillow fight" to her list and gave Peggy a cuddle. "Thanks, Peggy. I don't know what I'd do without you!"

At six o'clock the doorbell rang. Barking excitedly, Peggy ran to the door, wagging her curly tail.

"I'll get it!" cried Chloe, flinging the door open. Her friends Ellie and Hannah stepped inside, each holding a backpack and a sleeping bag.

"Hi, Peggy," said Hannah, crouching down to give her a pat. "Princess says hi." Princess was Hannah's pet dog. Peggy felt a bit sad that Princess wasn't coming to the sleepover, too, but the playful little terrier could be a bit naughty. It was probably for the best.

"Come on, guys," said Chloe. "Let's make pizzas!"

The girls headed into the kitchen. After washing their hands, they each took a small ball of the dough Dad had made earlier and rolled it out on the counter.

"Hey, watch this!" said Finn, coming into the kitchen. He picked up a circle of dough and tossed it in the air with a flourish.

PLOP! The dough landed on Peggy's head, covering her eyes.

"Help!" she barked. "I can't see!"

"Oops! Sorry, Peggy," said Finn, as he took the pizza dough off her head.

"I meant to catch that."

"*Muuuuummm!*" shouted Chloe. "Finn's pestering us!"

"It's OK," said Ellie. "He's funny."

"And kind of cute," Hannah whispered, blushing.

Looking horrified, Finn ran out of the kitchen.

"Well, *that* got rid of him," said Chloe.

The girls spread tomato sauce on their pizza bases, then sprinkled cheese and other tasty toppings on top. Peggy waited patiently by their feet, gobbling up any bits of cheese and pepperoni that fell on the floor.

After dinner, the girls and Peggy went

upstairs to Chloe's room. Giggling and singing along to pop music, they styled each other's hair and painted their nails. Peggy sniffed a bottle of hot pink nail polish curiously as Ellie plaited Chloe's hair.

"I think Peggy wants us to paint her claws," said Hannah, giggling.

"That wouldn't be good for her," said Chloe. "But we can do her hair."

Using a special grooming brush, the girls took it in turns to smooth down Peggy's soft, tan fur. *Ahhh, this is lovely,* Peggy thought happily. Then, as a finishing touch, Hannah clipped a pink bow on to her collar.

"You look gorgeous, Peggy," said Ellie.

"Let's get into our pyjamas," said Chloe. "And then we can watch a movie!"

The girls got changed and trooped downstairs into the living room with their pillows and sleeping bags. Mum and Dad were reading Ruby a story on the sofa, while Finn played a computer game.

"Ready for some popcorn?" asked Mum, looking up.

The girls nodded excitedly.

In the kitchen, Mum poured popcorn kernels into the popcorn maker and then – *POP! POP! POP!* – fluffy white popcorn came spluttering out of the machine.

"What are we going to watch?" asked Ellie, as they went back into the living room with a big bowl of buttery popcorn.

"How about *The Swamp Monster's Revenge*?" suggested Chloe, flicking through options on the screen with the remote control.

"Are you sure?" asked Finn, raising his eyebrow. "I've seen that – it's scary."

"We won't be scared," boasted Chloe.

"Can I watch too?" asked Ruby, yawning.

"It's time for you to go to bed," said Mum. "Come on – we'll tuck you in."

Once the others had left the room, Chloe and her friends switched off the lights, turned on the film, and snuggled up on the sofa with the bowl of popcorn between them. Chloe settled Peggy on her lap, and all three girls fed her pieces of popcorn as they watched the film.

Peggy liked the popcorn, but she didn't enjoy the movie. It was about a slimy green monster who lived in a lake and gobbled up anyone who went into the water. Peggy had to cover her eyes with her paws during all the scary bits. She could feel Chloe trembling, too.

As the movie neared the end, Peggy's ears pricked up. Something was creeping along the living room floor, slithering closer and closer. It was the swamp monster!

"*Raaaaaaaah!*" the monster roared,

reaching out a hand and grabbing Chloe's ankle.

The girls shrieked at the top of their lungs. Peggy knew she had to save them!

"Grrrrrrrr!" she growled, pouncing on the swamp monster.

"Calm down, Pegs," said a familiar voice. "It's just me."

Chloe turned on the light and revealed Finn, who was laughing so hard he could barely stand up.

"Ha! Ha! Ha!" gasped Finn, clutching his sides. "I thought you said you weren't going to be scared!"

"*Aaargh!* You are so annoying!" Chloe threw her pillow at her brother.

"Pillow fight!" cried Ellie, grabbing her pillow and flinging it at Finn.

He threw the pillow back at her, but missed and knocked over the bowl of popcorn.

"Take that!" shrieked Hannah, standing on the sofa and bopping Finn on the head with a cushion.

Soon, pillows and popcorn were flying all over the living room, as the children shrieked with laughter and Peggy ducked for cover. Suddenly, Mum and Dad appeared in the doorway in their dressing gowns, looking cross.

"OK, break it up," said Mum.

Dad sighed as he looked at the mess

on the floor. "I only just vacuumed this afternoon."

Wanting to be helpful, Peggy gobbled up as much of the popcorn from the floor as she could.

Dad switched off the television. "Time to get some sleep, kiddos."

"Awwww!" protested Chloe. "But it's not even midnight yet."

"Bedtime," Mum said firmly.

Once Mum, Dad and Finn had gone upstairs to bed, the girls spread their sleeping bags out on the living-room floor and climbed inside them. Peggy squeezed in between Chloe and Hannah. They were all snuggled up so close

Peggy could feel them breathing as they whispered secrets in the dark. It reminded her of when she was a puppy, nestled together with her brothers and sisters.

Sleepovers are fun! thought Peggy as she burrowed closer to Chloe. Then, closing her eyes, she fell into a deep, contented sleep.

Chapter Two

The next morning, Dad made pancakes
for breakfast. Then Ellie and Hannah got
dressed, rolled up their sleeping bags and
headed home. Peggy danced around by
the front door, whining. She wanted to
go out, too!

"Don't forget to take Peggy for her

morning walk," Dad reminded Chloe.

"But I'm *soooo* tired," said Chloe, yawning.

"That's what happens if you stay up half the night," said Dad, handing her Peggy's lead. "Actually, why don't you all go for a walk, while I hoover the living room floor AGAIN." He raised one eyebrow. "It somehow got covered with popcorn."

"Sorry, Dad," Chloe said, giggling.

"Let's go!" barked Peggy impatiently. She did *not* want to stick around if Dad was using the vacuum cleaner again!

"Why don't you pop in to see Mum?" added Dad. "She might need some help."

Peggy yapped excitedly. ran a café on the high street and Cups. It was a special dog- café, where dog owners could take their pets. Peggy loved going there!

Chloe, Finn and Ruby walked to the cafe together. Peggy liked the way the leaves crunched under her paws as she trotted along the pavement. She sniffed the crisp autumn air, smelling smoke wafting from a bonfire in a nearby garden.

"I can't wait for Halloween," said Finn.

"Me too," said Chloe. "I'm going trick-or-treating with Ellie and Hannah."

"We'll get lots of chocolate," said

Ruby, skipping along holding her big
brother's hand.

Hmm . . . Peggy wasn't sure she liked
the sound of trick-or-treating. Chocolate
was bad for dogs. She'd eaten some once
and got really ill.

When they reached the café, the bell
above the door jingled cheerfully as they
went inside.

"Hi, Dotty,"
Peggy
called to a
Dalmatian
whose
owner was
enjoying one

of Mum's delicious homemade cakes. "How are you?"

"Not bad," said Dotty, wagging her tail in greeting. "I've got a new toy." She gestured to the rubber chicken she'd been chewing on with her paw.

"Hi, guys," Mum said. "Could you help me put these up?" She handed Chloe a box of Halloween decorations. The children arranged little lights shaped like pumpkins around the display cabinet. Then Chloe dug some fake cobwebs and spiders out of the box.

"Ew," said Finn, recoiling from the spiders. "I'm not touching those." He hung a plastic skeleton on the front door, as Chloe and Ruby draped the fluffy cobwebs in the corners of the windows.

While the children decorated the café, Peggy made friends with a sausage dog named Lola, who was drinking from a water bowl while her owner read the newspaper.

"Thanks for your help," said Mum, giving the kids each a flapjack. Then she took the lid off a big glass jar. Peggy rushed over to her eagerly. She knew what that meant!

Mum reached into the jar and took out a dog biscuit. "And here's something for you, Peggy," she said, giving her the treat.

Yum! Peggy gobbled it up, wagging her tail happily.

On the way home, they cut through the park and Chloe let Peggy off her lead.

"Woo hoo!" cried Chloe, leaping into a huge pile of leaves. Finn and Ruby jumped in after her. Soon, all three children were laughing and frolicking together in the leaves.

Peggy wanted to play, too! She bounded after the children and jumped into the leaves . . . and sank right to the bottom of the pile!

Peggy's short legs paddled uselessly through the crunchy brown, red and gold leaves. They tickled her paws and went up her nose. She was completely buried – all she could see was leaves! "Help!" she yelped.

"I've got you, Peggy!" said Chloe, digging her out.

Phew!

Chloe held Peggy in her arms as they all flopped on their backs in the leaf pile, gazing up at the trees.

"Why do leaves change colour in autumn?" asked Ruby, holding up a pretty red maple leaf.

"When the weather gets colder, trees stop making something called chlorophyll," explained Finn. "That's the stuff that makes leaves green."

It wasn't just the trees getting ready for winter. Squirrels were scurrying about underneath the trees, looking for acorns to store up for the cold months ahead.

"It would be fun to live in a tree," said Ruby, as they watched a squirrel run up a tree trunk and disappear into a hollow.

"Yeah," agreed Chloe. "I've always wanted a tree house."

"I bet I could build one," said Finn. He was good at making things. He'd built a hutch for Coco, the family's pet rabbit. "My friends and I could use it as a secret hideout."

"Maybe you could move in for good," teased Chloe.

Finn threw some leaves at her. Giggling, Chloe threw a handful back at him. Ruby joined in the leaf fight, too. Barking happily, Peggy tried to catch the leaves in her mouth as they flew through the air. Soon, they were all panting.

"That was fun," said Chloe, brushing leaves off her clothes. Then she clipped Peggy's lead back on. They walked across the grass and left the park through the tall iron gates.

"That place always gives me the creeps," said Chloe, pointing to a big, old house right next to the park. The front gate was hanging off its hinges, the paint on the front door was peeling and the crumbling brickwork was covered in ivy. "Everyone says it's haunted."

Peggy's eyes widened in fear. A mournful noise seemed to be coming from the house. It sounded to her like a dog howling.

Chloe shivered. "I bet that's a ghost."

"Don't be stupid," scoffed Finn. "There's no such thing as ghosts."

But a furry white shape appeared briefly in one of the windows, before vanishing.

"Look!" said Chloe, pointing. "A ghost dog!"

A ghost dog! thought Peggy, all of her fur standing on end. She whimpered and strained on her lead. *Let's get out of here!*

"Come on," said Chloe. "Peggy wants to go."

When they got back home, Finn asked Dad if he could build a tree house.

"Sure," said Dad. "There should be

some wood in the shed."

"Want to help me plan my design?" Finn asked his sisters.

"Me!" said Ruby eagerly. "I will!"

But Chloe shook her head. "I've got to do my homework. I'm supposed to write a spooky story for a Halloween writing competition."

Upstairs, Chloe got out her sparkly notebook. "I don't know what to write about, Peggy," she said, drumming her pen against the cover.

Peggy licked Chloe's face to give her some encouragement.

"I know!" Chloe said, her eyes lighting up. "I'll write about a dog!"

Great idea!
thought Peggy.

As Chloe began
to write her story,
Peggy yawned
and stretched out

on Chloe's duvet. Then she rested her
head on her front paws and closed her
eyes. Sleepovers were fun, but they *did*
make you very tired the next day!

That night, after dinner, Chloe read her
story to her family. It was about a white
dog who fell into a lake when its owner

wasn't paying attention and got gobbled up by a hideous swamp monster. Then it came back as a vicious ghost dog to haunt the old house where it had lived.

Peggy shivered as she listened to the story. The house sounded a lot like the one near the park – the one with the ghost dog!

"I love it," said Mum.

"You have a wonderful imagination," said Dad.

"It's really scary," said Ruby, her eyes wide.

Chloe beamed proudly.

"It would be even scarier if the ghost dog had fangs like a vampire," suggested

Finn. "And it wanted to drink people's blood."

"Ooh! That's a great idea," said Chloe, quickly adding a few more lines to her story.

That night in bed, snuggled up next to Chloe, who was snoring softly, Peggy couldn't fall asleep. Every time she closed her eyes, she thought about Chloe's spooky story. And in the distance, she could hear a faint howling noise.

Peggy shuddered. Was it the wind? Or was it the ghost dog, wailing in the night?

CREEEAAAAAK!

Peggy's ears pricked up. She lifted her

head up and and listened carefully. There was the creaking noise again! It was coming from somewhere nearby. . .

Peggy wanted to hide under the bed, but she knew she had to be brave. What if a ghost was sneaking up on her family? She had to protect Chloe, Ruby and Finn!

Summoning all her courage, Peggy climbed off the bed and padded out of the bedroom. In the dark hallway, Peggy saw a menacing-looking shape. Was it a ghost?

She nudged it with her paw. No, it was just the laundry hamper.

Suddenly, a door opened slowly ...

The ghost is coming!

Peggy growled and got ready to pounce.

"Shhhhh!" whispered Dad, stepping out of the bathroom. "It's just me. I needed the loo."

He picked Peggy up and carried her back to Chloe's room, setting her down

on the bed. "Sweet dreams," he said,
patting her head.

But even snuggled up close to Chloe,
Peggy couldn't sleep a wink.

Chapter Three

"Right!" said Dad, rubbing his hands.
"Let's go and harvest some pumpkins!"

They were all outside in their welly
boots the next day. Dad opened the shed
and they helped him gather up some
gardening tools.

Peggy liked it in the shed. It was

filled with all sorts of interesting things – bicycles, garden furniture and a snow shovel. She gave a big bag of wood shavings a curious sniff. They smelled like Coco's hutch.

"I'm going to make a jack-o'-lantern!" said Chloe as Dad handed her a spade.

"What's a jack-o'-lantern?" asked Ruby.

"It's when you carve a face into a pumpkin," explained Chloe. "And then you put a candle or a light inside it to make a lantern."

"I want to make one too!" cried Ruby.

"You can each pick a pumpkin to carve," said Dad.

"Hey, Dad," said Finn, holding up a plank of wood. "Can I use this for my tree house?"

"Sure," said Dad. "You can use anyth—"

"*Eeeeek!*" screamed Finn, dropping the wood and jumping back in fright. "A spider!"

Chloe giggled. "A spider can't hurt you."

Finn shuddered. "They're so hairy and crawly."

How silly, thought Peggy, watching the spider scurry away into a corner of the shed.

"Spiders are great for the garden," said

Dad. "They eat all sorts of insects that damage plants."

"I don't care," said Finn. "They're horrible."

"Sorry," Peggy called over to the spider. "He doesn't mean to be rude."

"No worries," said the spider, peeping out from under another plank of wood. "I get that a lot."

"Well, you're going to have to face

your fears if you want to use the wood," Dad told Finn. "Because spiders love it in here."

Dad led the kids over to his vegetable patch. There was a little fence all around it to separate the neat rows of plants from the rest of the garden. Peggy tried to follow them in.

"No, Peggy," said Dad firmly. "You can't come in here."

Not fair, Peggy thought. OK, so she'd dug up Dad's vegetable patch that one time. She knew better than to do it again.

"You can hang out with Coco," said Chloe, pulling a carrot out of the soil.

Brushing dirt off it, she took Peggy over to the rabbit hutch. Then, popping the carrot inside, Chloe went back to the vegetable patch.

"Hi, Coco," said Peggy.

"Hi, Peggy," said the little black and white rabbit. "You look tired."

"I *am* tired," Peggy admitted. "I didn't get much sleep last night." She suddenly realised something: Coco slept outside, alone in her hutch. "Don't you get scared out here at night, all by yourself?"

"Oh no," said Coco. "I'm used to it. It's beautiful at night. I like listening to the owls hooting, and gazing up at the moon and stars. Sometimes I even see comets shooting across the sky."

Wow, thought Peggy. Coco was clearly braver than she looked.

"If you're not scared of the dark, what *are* you scared of?" Peggy asked the bunny.

"*Hmm,*" said Coco, twitching her

pink nose thoughtfully. Then her eyes
widened in fear and her whiskers
trembled. "Cats!"

Peggy turned and saw Tiger, the
neighbour's stripy ginger cat, stalking
through the grass. She groaned.

"Hello, Pig Tail," the mean old cat
purred. He grinned slyly at Coco,
showing his sharp teeth. "You're looking
very tasty today, Long Ears."

Coco trembled in
her hutch.

"Don't worry,
Coco," Peggy
said. "He can't
hurt you."

Suddenly, Peggy heard a mournful howl in the distance.

ARRROOOOOOOOOO!

"Did you hear that?" Peggy asked.

Coco and Tiger nodded.

"I think it might be a ghost dog," said Peggy. "Have either of you ever seen a ghost?"

"Oh yes," said Tiger, licking his paws. "Many times. And witches, too."

"Witches?" said Peggy nervously.

"You see lots of witches on Halloween night," said Tiger. "You can hear them cackling as they fly through the air on their broomsticks. Most of them have a black cat riding on the back." His green eyes glittered mischievously.

Peggy gasped. Witches sounded even scarier than monsters and ghosts!

"You'd better watch out, Pig Tail," Tiger said to Peggy. "Because curly little pug tails are witches' favourite ingredient to put in their magic spells."

"You're making that up!" Peggy said.

The cat sauntered over to the fence. "Well, don't blame me if your tail ends up in a witch's cauldron. I tried to warn you," he said. Then he leaped up and disappeared over the fence.

"Tiger's just teasing you," said Coco. "You know what he's like."

"Maybe . . ." Peggy glanced behind

her nervously, trying to see her tail. She didn't want to take any chances!

"Peggy!" called Chloe. "Come and see our pumpkins!"

Peggy bounded across the garden to her friend, who was holding a perfectly round, orange pumpkin in her arms.

"Mine's only little," said Ruby. "Just like me!"

"Let's take these inside before my arms break," said Finn, staggering under the weight of an enormous pumpkin covered in bumps that looked like warts.

Inside, Mum spread newspaper on the kitchen table, and they all set to work decorating their pumpkins. Ruby decided to draw hearts and flowers on hers.

"That's lovely, Rubes," said Mum, helping her carve out the shapes with the sharp knife.

"Jack-o'-lanterns are supposed to be scary," said Finn. "Not pretty." He cut out the top of his pumpkin and scraped out the stringy insides with a spoon.

Some of the slimy seeds fell on the floor.
Peggy tried to eat one but quickly spat it
out.

Pumpkin seeds were horrible, but not
as horrible as Finn's jack-o'-lantern. It
had sharp, jagged fangs, a triangle nose
and narrow, glaring eyes. Finn scooped
up some of the slimy pumpkin seeds and
made it look like the jack-o'-lantern was
throwing up.

Yikes, thought Peggy. It gave her the
creeps.

"That's disgusting," said Chloe.

"Why thank you very much," said
Finn proudly.

Chloe had scraped out the inside of her

pumpkin, too, but she hadn't started to decorate it yet.

"What are you going to do, Chloe?" asked Mum.

"I haven't decided," said Chloe, frowning at her pumpkin. "I want it to be really special."

"I want to help!" said Peggy, jumping

up on to Chloe's lap and giving the pumpkin an inquisitive lick. Nope – the outside didn't taste any nicer than the inside!

Chloe stroked Peggy's fur as she continued to stare at her pumpkin. "I know!" she suddenly exclaimed. "I'm going to make mine a pug!"

Chloe carved two big eyes, floppy ears and a flat nose. Then she used a black marker to draw on whiskers.

"That's great," said Mum. "It looks just like Peggy."

Except I'm much *cuter,* thought Peggy.

"Hey, Mum!" said Chloe, her eyes glowing with excitement. "We should have a Halloween party at the café, and owners can come with their dogs!"

"Yay!" said Ruby, clapping her hands in delight. "I love parties!"

Finn nodded. "That would be pretty cool."

Peggy looked at Mum expectantly. A party at Pups and Cups *did* sound fun.

Mum smiled. "That's a fantastic idea!" she said.

"Yay! We're having a pug-o-ween party!" said Chloe, giving Peggy a hug.

Chapter Four

"Come outside, you guys," said Finn,
bursting into the living room where
Chloe and Ruby were watching
Sparkalina, their favourite TV show, about
a magical unicorn. Peggy was curled
up on Chloe's lap. She loved watching
Sparkalina too!

Nobody moved.

"The episode just started," said Chloe.

"We've never seen this one," said Ruby.

I'm too comfy, thought Peggy.

Finn stood in front of the television, blocking the screen. "Then I guess you don't want to try out the tree house . . ."

"Is it finished?" Ruby asked excitedly.

Finn nodded.

Chloe pushed Peggy off her lap and sprang up.

"Hey!" yelped Peggy indignantly. She took one last backwards glance at *Sparkalina,* then followed the kids as they ran into the garden.

Finn had been busy working on the

tree house for days. He'd built a platform in the fork of the big oak tree at the end of the garden. The walls and roof, made from odd planks of wood nailed together, were partly hidden by the branches. A painted sign that read "Private – Keep Out!" was nailed to the door.

"Wow!" said Chloe. "It looks amazing!"

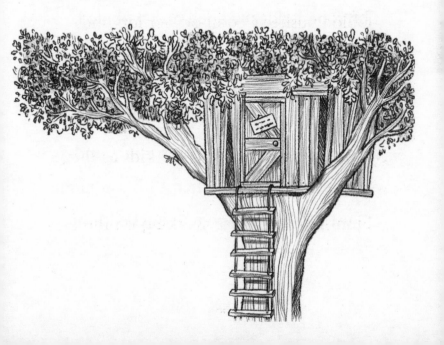

Finn climbed up a rope ladder and stuck his head out of the doorway. "Come on up!" he called down to his sisters.

Chloe quickly scrambled up the ladder. "It's so cool!" She beckoned to her little sister from the tree house. "Hurry up, Ruby."

Ruby put her foot on the bottom rung. The rope ladder swayed and wobbled.

"I can't," she wailed, shaking her head.

"Don't be scared, Rubes," said Finn. "I promise it's safe."

Ruby climbed up another rung, and clung to the rope, terrified. "It's too high."

"Just don't look down," coached Finn.

Peggy reached up with her front paw and gently nudged Ruby. "Go on," she barked encouragingly. "You can do it."

Ruby took a deep breath. "OK," she said bravely. "I'm coming up."

Finn reached down and helped pull his little sister into the tree house as she reached the top.

"You made it!" cheered Chloe.

"I'm going to decorate the tree house for Halloween," said Finn. "It will be a haunted tree house."

"No!" barked Peggy. Why did everything have to be spooky?

"I think Peggy wants to come up, too," said Ruby.

"We could put her in a basket and pull it up with a rope," suggested Finn.

"Don't even think about it!" Peggy barked loudly. Trees were for squirrels and birds – not dogs!

"Actually, I think she wants to go for a walk," said Chloe.

Now you're talking . . . thought Peggy.

Chloe climbed down the rope ladder and fetched Peggy's lead. Then they walked down the street towards the park.

MEOOOWWW!

A little black cat was sunning herself on a garden wall. She meowed at them as they walked past. Remembering what Tiger had told her about witches' cats,

Peggy yelped and hid behind Chloe's legs. She didn't want her tail to end up in a witch's cauldron!

As they got close to the park, Peggy heard the howling noise again. It was coming from the haunted house near the park.

Peggy planted her feet on the ground, refusing to go any further.

"Come on, Peggy," said Chloe, tugging on her lead. "Don't be silly."

"*Nooooo!*" wailed Peggy, trying to go back home. What if the ghost dog attacked them?

"You are acting so weird today," Chloe said. She scooped Peggy up into her arms and carried her into the park. "I told my friends I'd meet them in the playground."

When they got to the playground, Ellie and Hannah were already there. The playground was empty, apart from one other girl with short, curly hair and glasses, who was on a swing. Peggy cheered up a bit as she spotted her friend, Princess.

Chloe set Peggy down on the ground and unclipped her lead so the two little dogs could play together.

"Hi, Peggy," said Princess, wagging her tail as they touched noses in greeting. "Before you say it, I know I look ridiculous." Today Princess was wearing a leopard-print coat with a matching bow in her hair. "I mean, really. Why would you dress a dog up like a cat? It's so humiliating."

"Guess what?" Chloe said to her friends. "We're having a pug-o-ween

party at my mum's café and you're both invited!"

"Pug-o-ween?" asked Ellie, confused.

"It's a Halloween party," explained Chloe. "But people can bring their dogs."

"Ooh!" said Hannah. "That sounds so fun! Princess and I can both be demon cheerleaders!"

"Oh, good grief," said Princess, rolling

her eyes. "Another ridiculous outfit."

"What are you going to dress up as?"
Hannah asked the others.

"I haven't decided yet," said Chloe.

"Well, you'd better hurry up," said
Hannah. "Halloween's only a few days
away."

"I'm going to be a vampire," said Ellie.
She put on a creepy voice and held up
her hands like claws. "*I vant to suck your
blood!*"

Chloe and Hannah squealed as Ellie
chased them around the park, pretending
to be a vampire. Peggy and Princess
played together, too. They rolled in the
crunchy fallen leaves and took turns

chasing each other around the grass.

Peggy was running to catch Princess when she noticed a flash of white out of the corner of her eye. She turned and saw a huge, white dog with shaggy fur peeping out from behind a bush. Its blue eyes stared back at her.

The ghost dog!

Peggy froze, too scared to move a muscle.

"What's wrong?" asked Princess, bounding up.

"Look!" whispered Peggy.

"OK. But what am I supposed to be looking at?" asked Princess, gazing around, confused.

Peggy blinked. The ghost dog had
vanished. She looked all around, but
there was nobody in the playground
– even the girl on the swings had gone.
She ran over to the bush to investigate.
There were paw prints in the dirt, but
there was no sign of the ghost dog
anywhere.

"I saw it a second ago," she told

Princess. "And then it disappeared."

"Saw what?" said Princess.

"The ghost dog!" said Peggy.

"Ghost dog?" laughed Princess. "What are you on about?"

"I saw it the other day, too," insisted Peggy. "In the window of the haunted house."

"You're just imagining things," said Princess, shaking her head. "Because you've got Halloween on the brain."

But Peggy knew what she had seen. And now she was more scared than ever!

Chapter Five

A terrible banging and twanging sound
woke Peggy from her nap the next
afternoon. Someone was wailing, too.
Was the ghost dog howling again? She
cocked her head to the side and listened.
This sounded different – and closer.
Much, much closer . . .

Peggy jumped down from Chloe's bed and went downstairs. The back door was ajar, so she slipped outside. Following the sound, which was getting louder and louder, Peggy crept over to the garage to investigate.

Peering inside, she gasped. A zombie, a skeleton and a ghost were singing and dancing around the garage!

"*Oooooo, I wanna give you a fright!*" wailed the zombie.

"*On Halloween night!*" chorused the skeleton and ghost.

Panicking, Peggy turned and ran away. She cowered behind the rabbit hutch, trembling. This wasn't good at all. One monster was bad enough – but how could she possibly take on *three* of them?

"What's wrong, Peggy?" asked Coco, hopping over and pressing her pink nose against the hutch's wire mesh window.

"Shhh!" hissed Peggy urgently. "They'll hear you!"

"Who will hear me?" asked Coco.

"The ghouls in the garage. I've got to warn the others—"

The wailing suddenly stopped. Peggy's heart pounded with fear. Had the zombie spotted her? Was it coming to eat her brains?

"Is that who you mean?" asked Coco.

Peggy turned and whimpered. The

zombie was heading straight towards
them – with the skeleton and ghost right
behind him!

Shaking with fright, Peggy squeezed
her eyes shut, bracing herself for the
worst.

"Check this out," said a familiar voice.

Huh? Peggy opened one eye and saw the zombie peel off his face . . . then she let out a sigh of relief.

"This is the tree house I built," Finn said proudly, holding the scary zombie mask he'd been wearing in his hand.

"Oh, wow," said the skeleton, looking up at the tree house. As it came closer, Peggy recognised Jasmine, the keyboard player in Finn's band. "It's wicked!"

"It can be our band headquarters," said Finn. He'd decorated the tree house with his scary jack-o'-lantern and some bright yellow tape that said "Danger – Crime Scene!"

The ghost approached and crouched

down in front of Peggy. Was this the
ghost she'd heard howling? She growled
and sank her teeth into its billowing
white form.

"Oi, let go!" said the ghost.

But Peggy held on tight and tugged.
She wasn't going to let it get away!
A white sheet pooled on the ground,
revealing a friendly face underneath it.

Oh, thought Peggy. It wasn't a ghost
after all. It was just Zack – the band's
guitar player.

"Do you like our Halloween costumes,
Peggy?" he asked, patting her on the
head.

"We're a *death* metal band," said Finn,

laughing. "Get it?"

"Our new song totally rocks!" said Jasmine.

"Do you really think your mum will let us play at the Halloween party?" asked Zack.

"Come on," said Finn. "Let's go and ask her."

"See, Peggy," said Coco, as the band trooped into the house. "There's nothing to worry about."

Feeling a bit silly, Peggy followed the band inside. Mum was in the kitchen, where Chloe and Ruby were helping her bake. The kitchen counter was covered in flour – and so was Ruby.

"How was your rehearsal?" said Mum, taking a tray of pumpkin-shaped cookies out of the oven. "You sounded good out there."

Chloe grinned as she pressed out more pumpkin shapes with a cutter. "I thought that was Tiger yowling," she teased her brother.

Finn reached over and helped himself to some biscuits cooling on a wire rack, handing them out to his bandmates.

"No more," said Mum, rapping Finn's hand lightly with a wooden spoon. "Those are for the pug-o-ween party."

"These are really good," said Zack.

"Hey, Mum," said Finn, sharing a

piece of his biscuit with Peggy. "We were wondering if we could play a few songs at the party."

"Sure," Mum said. "That's fine."

"Woo hoo!" cheered the band, giving each other high fives.

"We're going to play games, too," said Chloe. "Bobbing for apples . . . pin the tail on the witch's cat . . . mummy wrap—"

"How do you play that?" asked Zack.

Chloe ran to the bathroom and came back with a roll of toilet paper. "I'll show you!" she said. Then she wound toilet paper all around him, wrapping him up like an Egyptian mummy. The others laughed as Zack pretended to be a mummy, his arms stretched out in front of him.

"I'm not going to be a mummy for Halloween," said Ruby. "I'm going to be a witch." She grabbed a broom from the cupboard, stuck it between her legs, and ran around the kitchen cackling. Coming to a stop in front of Peggy, she said, "You can be my witch's cat!" She

took off her hairband, which had cat ears on it, and stuck it on Peggy's head.

"No way!" barked Peggy, shaking her head to get the cat ears off. She didn't even want to go trick-or-treating – and certainly not as a witch's cat!

"What's your costume going to be, Chloe?" asked Jasmine.

"I still haven't decided," said Chloe.

"I've got a witch costume you could borrow," Jasmine offered.

Chloe shook her head. "I don't want to copy Ruby."

"Just go as yourself," teased Finn. "Your face will scare people just as it is."

"Oh, ha ha," said Chloe, sticking out

her tongue at her brother.

"A ghost costume is easy to make," said Zack. "You just need to cut some holes in a sheet."

Chloe wrinkled her nose. "I was a ghost last year."

The kids all sneaked another biscuit behind Mum's back. When she turned around, there were only a few biscuits left on the cooling rack. She chuckled. "Oh dear, looks like I'm going to have to bake another batch."

"Sorry, Mum," said Chloe, brushing crumbs off her mouth. "They're just *sooooo* good."

"Go and fetch me another pumpkin

from the garden," said Mum.

"Come with me, Peggy," said Chloe, patting her thighs.

Peggy trotted after her eagerly, relieved to get away from all the Halloween talk.

Chloe went into the vegetable patch and peered under the leaves, looking for a ripe pumpkin. "Ooh, this one looks good," she said, cutting a plump, round pumpkin off its vine.

"What do you think, Peggy?" she asked, brushing dirt off the pumpkin and holding it up.

Peggy gave a bark of approval.

"Oh my goodness!" exclaimed Chloe. "I've just had the best idea – we can both be PUMPKINS for Halloween and go trick-or-treating together!"

What?

Peggy stared at Chloe in disbelief. That wasn't the best idea ever – it was the worst.

She didn't want to be a pumpkin. She didn't want to dress up in any costume at all.

Because Peggy wanted to spend Halloween night at home, hiding under the bed!

Chapter Six

The next afternoon, Peggy pressed her nose against the front window, waiting eagerly for the children to come home from school. Now there were more leaves on the ground than on the tree branches, and a patchwork quilt of red, yellow and brown leaves covered the lawn. When she caught a glimpse of Chloe and Ruby walking down the street, Peggy's tail began to wag excitedly. *They're almost home!*

The house was too quiet when the children were at school and Mum was at the café. Dad worked from home and usually took Peggy for a walk at lunchtime, but most of the day he was busy tapping away on his laptop in the office upstairs. There wasn't much for Peggy to do but take naps, play with her chew toys and chat to Coco in the back garden. It sometimes got a bit boring.

As soon as she heard Chloe's key in the lock, Peggy ran into the hallway.

But when the girls came in, she could tell that something was wrong. Chloe's face usually lit up when she saw Peggy, but today she wasn't smiling. She dropped her schoolbag on to the ground and bent down to pick Peggy up.

"Oh, Peggy," she said, rubbing her cheek against Peggy's fur. "I had the worst day."

And then she began to cry.

Oh no! thought Peggy. She hated to see Chloe upset! She licked the tears rolling down her friend's cheeks, wishing she could cheer her up.

"Daddy!" called Ruby.

Dad hurried downstairs.

"What's wrong?" he asked.

Chloe opened her mouth, but she was crying too hard to get any words out. She just  clung to Peggy and sobbed.

"Did she get hurt on the walk home?" Dad asked Ruby.

"No." Ruby shook her head solemnly. "But she was really sad the whole way home from school."

"What is it, sweetheart?" Dad asked

Chloe, crouching down so he could look in her eyes. "Please tell me. I can't help you if I don't know what's wrong."

Ruby went into the bathroom and came back with a tissue for her sister. Chloe set Peggy down on the ground so she could wipe her eyes and blow her nose. Then she took a deep breath and said in a shaky voice: "My spooky story won first prize in the competition."

"But that's wonderful news!" said Dad, confused.

"No, it's not!" wailed Chloe. "It means I have to read it out loud to the whole school in assembly!" She promptly burst into tears again.

Dad hugged Chloe and stroked her back. "Oh, honey," he said soothingly. "You should feel proud, not upset. This is really exciting."

Chloe shook her head. "I can't do it! There will be so many kids staring at me. I hate speaking in front of an audience."

"But your story is really good, Chloe," said Ruby. "Everyone will love it."

"I used to hate giving presentations," said Dad. "But I have to do it for my work. Shall I tell you a little trick I use?"

Chloe nodded tearfully.

Dad dropped his voice to a whisper. "I pretend everyone in the audience is in their underwear."

The corners of Chloe's mouth twitched into a faint smile.

"I bet Mr Sanders the headteacher wears saggy baggy underpants!" said Ruby.

"Ew," said Chloe, but she giggled.

"I promise it helps," said Dad. "And you can practise on us. We'd love to hear your story again."

Peggy gave a little bark and wagged her tail. Chloe's story had scared her, but she was willing to help her friend any way she could.

Ruby fished out something made from black pipe cleaners from her school bag. "Look what I made," she said proudly,

holding it out on her palm. "It's a spider."

"That's really cute," said Chloe.

"You can have it," said Ruby, handing
it to her.

"Aw, thanks," said Chloe, giving her
little sister a hug.

"Does anyone want a snack?" asked
Dad.

"Me!" cried Chloe and Ruby together.

"Me!" barked Peggy. That was another reason she was always happy when the children came home from school – snack time! She trailed after them and waited patiently as Dad gave the girls each a biscuit and an apple.

"Hey – what about me?" barked Peggy.

Dad reached into a jar of dog biscuits. "Peggy – sit," he said.

Oh all right, thought Peggy, sighing. *If you insist.* She sat down obediently, never taking her eyes off the dog treat.

Dad rewarded her with the dog biscuit, which Peggy bolted down in one bite.

Dee-lish!

As the girls munched their apples, Chloe said, "I think we've got some pipe cleaners in the craft box. Maybe we should make some more spider decorations for the party tomorrow."

Peggy gulped nervously. She'd almost forgotten it was Halloween tomorrow. She'd been doing her best not to think about witches, ghosts and monsters. Chloe hadn't said anything more about both of them being pumpkins, and Peggy really hoped she had given up on the idea.

Chloe got out the craft box and found some black pipe cleaners. As the girls made spiders, twisting the pipe cleaners into eight long legs and gluing on googly eyes, they talked about the party.

"It's going to be so great," said Chloe. "Finn's band are working on some spooky new songs."

"Mummy said there's going to be a prize for the creepiest costume," said Ruby.

The more she heard about the pug-o-ween party, the more anxious Peggy felt. Maybe she could do something to stop it from going ahead?

I know! she thought. *I'll spoil the decorations!* She climbed up on to Chloe's lap and squashed one of the spiders with her paw.

"Naughty, Peggy," said Chloe, taking the spider away. She set Peggy down on the ground and fixed the spider's legs.

Humph! thought Peggy. She'd just have to think of a new plan . . .

Chloe rummaged in the craft box again and found some white tissue paper. "We could make some ghosts out of this," she said. "We just need tennis balls."

"I've got some," said Dad, who was chopping vegetables for dinner. "They're in my sports bag in the cupboard under the stairs."

When Chloe came back with the tennis balls, Peggy had a great idea. *I'll distract them!*

Jumping up, she grabbed a tennis ball in her mouth. She rushed to the back door, wagging her tail, hoping her friend would get the hint.

"No, Peggy," said Chloe, taking the ball out of Peggy's mouth and wiping it off. "I can't play fetch. We're making Halloween decorations."

Aww . . . Defeated, Peggy flopped down on her belly.

She watched as the girls covered the tennis balls with white tissue paper, which they tied off with a bit of string. Then they used a black marker pen to draw eyes and an O-shaped mouth on the ghosts.

What a waste of perfectly good tennis balls, thought Peggy grumpily, imagining all the fun they could be having playing fetch in the garden.

Her ears perked up as she heard someone at the door.

"That will be Finn," said Dad, draining spaghetti in the colander.

Because he was older, Finn went to a different school to Ruby and Chloe. He stayed late sometimes, for band practice or a football match.

"Quick!" whispered Chloe, grinning mischievously. "Let's play a trick on him!" She put one of the pipe-cleaner spiders on his chair. Ruby covered her mouth, trying not to laugh.

A few moments later, Finn came into the kitchen in his muddy football gear. "Phew!" he said. "We won, but I'm exhausted." He dropped his kit bag on the floor, flopped down in his chair – then jumped right back up again.

"*Aaarggghhh!*" he screamed, looking down at the spider. Then, realising it was fake, he flung it at his giggling sisters.

"We tricked you!" squealed Ruby, dancing around the kitchen.

"I knew it wasn't real," said Finn. "I was just pretending to be scared."

"Yeah, right," said Chloe, grinning.

As Finn did his maths homework, the girls made more ghosts, until they'd used up all the tennis balls.

"Oh, I forgot. I've got a surprise for you," said Finn, closing his maths book.

"What is it?" asked Chloe suspiciously.

"You'll see," said Finn. "But first – close your eyes. And no peeking!"

The girls shut their eyes.

Peggy watched curiously as Finn tiptoed over to the counter and picked up the colander of spaghetti. "Hold out your hands . . ." he instructed his sisters, who did as they were told. "NOW FEEL THE ZOMBIE BRAINS!" Finn shouted, shoving their hands into the spaghetti.

Ruby and Chloe squealed and pulled their hands away. When they opened their eyes, Finn was laughing. "I got you back!"

Chloe flung a piece of spaghetti at him.

"Give me that," said Dad, taking the colander of spaghetti off Finn. "Now go and change out of that filthy kit before dinner."

"We should definitely do that at the

party," said Chloe. "We can have other gross stuff too – peeled grapes can be monster eyeballs."

"Carrots can be witches' fingers," suggested Ruby.

"And jelly can be mummy guts," said Chloe.

Ugh, thought Peggy. Even though the pasta Dad was cooking for dinner smelled yummy, she'd suddenly lost her appetite.

When Mum came home from the café, Chloe told her about her story winning the competition and showed her the decorations they had made.

"That's brilliant," said Mum. "I've

got something to show you, too." She
reached into the carrier bag she was
holding and pulled out a pumpkin
costume. "This is for you, Chloe."

"Thanks, Mum," said Chloe, beaming.
"It's perfect!"

Phew! thought Peggy. There was only
one costume. Maybe she wouldn't have
to be a pumpkin, after all.

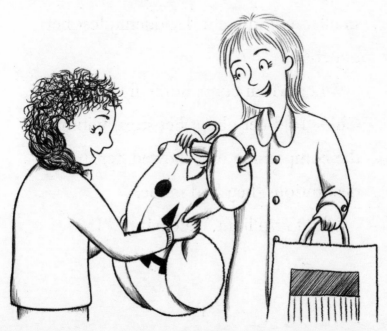

But then Mum reached into her bag again, and pulled out a pug-sized pumpkin costume. "And this one is for Peggy!"

Oh dear . . .

Chapter Seven

On Halloween morning, Peggy licked Chloe's face to wake her up. But instead of hopping out of bed, Chloe rolled over and pulled the pillow over her head. "I don't want to go to school today," she groaned. "I'm supposed to read my story in assembly."

But Peggy wanted her breakfast. She tugged the pillow off Chloe's face.

"Maybe I can pretend to be sick," Chloe said. She sat up and coughed a few times, then collapsed back on her pillow, one hand flung across her forehead.

Very convincing! thought Peggy happily. If Chloe stayed home from school, they could snuggle on the sofa and watch *Sparkalina* all day long.

Chloe sighed. "But if I don't go to school, Mum won't let me go to the party – or trick-or-treating."

Exactly! Peggy didn't want to do either of those things.

To Peggy's disappointment, Chloe pushed the covers off and got out of bed. She dressed for school then they both went downstairs, where the rest of the family was eating breakfast.

"Happy Halloween," said Mum.

"I made you some toast with peanut butter," said Dad.

"I'm too nervous to eat," said Chloe. She sat with Peggy on her lap, stroking her with trembling hands.

"Why don't you read us your story to practise?" suggested Mum.

"OK," said Chloe. She took her story out of her school bag, cleared her throat and read the story about the ghost dog to the others. It was still just as scary as Peggy remembered. There was a slight quaver in her friend's voice at first, but as she read, her voice grew more and more confident. When she finally said, "The End", everyone clapped.

"That was pretty good," said Finn, helping himself to Chloe's uneaten toast.

"Remember," said Dad. "Just picture everyone in their underwear."

"I'm wearing ones with blue stars on them," whispered Ruby, giggling.

"I'd better hurry up and get to the café," said Mum, checking her watch. She gathered up the Halloween decorations the girls had made the day before. Then she gave Chloe a kiss goodbye. "Be brave, sweetheart. I'll see you at the party later on."

The party! Peggy's tummy flip-flopped with fear.

"You, too, Peggy," said Mum, giving

her a pat on the head.

After the children left for school, Peggy went into the garden. She could hear a mournful howl coming from down the street. Peggy's fur stood on end as she listened to it and thought about the scary ghost dog in Chloe's story. What if it attacked her when they were trick-or-treating? She shuddered. She *had* to find some way to avoid going out tonight!

"What's wrong, Peggy?" asked Coco.

"Today's Halloween," said Peggy. "I'm supposed to go to the party at Mum's café."

"What will you do there?" asked Coco.

"There will be games, music and snacks and everyone will be wearing costumes – even the dogs," said Peggy.

"That sounds really fun," said Coco wistfully. "I wish I could go."

Hmm, thought Peggy. Was there some way she and Coco could swap places just for tonight? Maybe Coco could wear the pumpkin costume instead. No, that wouldn't work. The costume would be much too big on Coco. Besides, not all dogs were as friendly with bunnies as she was ...

There was a sound behind her and Peggy was so startled she nearly jumped a foot in the air.

Heart racing, she turned and said, "Oh, Tiger! You scared me."

"Can you feel the Halloween magic?" hissed the cat, twitching his tail from side to side. "The witches are getting ready to ride tonight, so you'd better watch out, Pig Tail."

"You're just trying to scare me," Peggy

said, hoping she sounded braver than she felt.

"Oh, really," said Tiger, narrowing his eyes at her. He nodded at a creature with bulging eyes and bumpy skin who was hopping through the vegetable patch. "Do you know what that is?"

"A toad?" said Peggy uncertainly. Or was it a frog? She could never tell the difference.

"It is now," said Tiger. "But it used to be a cute little cocker spaniel named Maisy. She crossed paths with a witch on Halloween night and her tail ended up in a cauldron. The witch didn't need her after that so – abracadabra, hey presto –

she turned her into a toad."

Peggy's eyes widened as she stared at the toad in horror. Had it really once been a dog?

"Hello, Maisy," she whispered.

The toad croaked loudly in reply.

Oh no, thought Peggy. *Poor Maisy.*

"Tiger's just teasing you," said Coco.

But Peggy didn't want to take any

chances. "Gotta go!" she said, and dashed back into the house.

When the girls came home from school that afternoon, Chloe was clutching a little gold trophy.

"How did it go?" Dad asked her.

"Really well," said Chloe, smiling so widely Peggy could see the gap at the back where she'd lost a tooth a few weeks before. She held up the trophy. "I got this."

"Chloe was amazing," said Ruby proudly. "Josh in my class was so scared by Chloe's story that he ran out of the hall crying. What a baby!"

"I pictured everyone in their underwear," said Chloe. "It really helped."

"Told you!" said Dad, giving her a high five.

When Finn came back from school, the

children went upstairs and started getting ready for the pug-o-ween party.

"*Oooo, I want to give you a fright,*" sang Finn. Peggy peeped into his bedroom and saw him putting on his zombie costume, which was a tattered grey suit. Then he put on his horrible rubber mask. It had wild grey hair, dark rings around the eyes, and blood dripping from the mouth.

Yuck! Peggy hurried away, not wanting to look. She stopped outside the bathroom. Chloe was wearing her bright orange pumpkin costume. There was a little green hat like a stem on her head, and she had on matching green tights.

She was painting Ruby's face with green make-up.

When Chloe was finished, Ruby put on her pointy black witch's hat and looked in the mirror. "I'm going to get you, my pretty, and your little dog too!" she said, cackling.

That's it! thought Peggy. *I'm out of here!*

She hurried down the hallway and hid inside Chloe's wardrobe, curling up in a ball on a pile of soft jumpers. *They'll never find me here!*

Not long afterwards, Chloe came looking for her. "Peggy!" she called. "Where are you?"

Peggy peeped out of the wardrobe

and saw Chloe holding the pug-sized pumpkin costume.

"It's time to get ready for the party, Peggy!" Frowning, Chloe looked under the bed.

Peggy held her breath, not daring to move a muscle. If Chloe found her, she'd have to go to the party!

Dad, who was dressed like a scarecrow, came into Chloe's bedroom. "We've got to go now," he said. "The party's starting soon."

"But I can't find Peggy," said Chloe.

"We'll just have to leave her at home, then," said Dad.

"But it's a *pug*-o-ween party," said

Chloe. "It won't be any fun if Peggy isn't
there. Maybe I won't go . . ."

Peggy felt a twinge of guilt. Chloe
sounded so sad. As she peered out, a glint
of gold caught her eye. It was the trophy
Chloe had won for her story. Peggy
thought of how courageous Chloe had
been today. She'd been terrified about

reading her story out in front of all the
other children, but she'd overcome her
fears and done it.

Chloe was really brave, Peggy thought. *So
I need to be brave, too.*

Peggy was scared to go out tonight.
But she didn't want Chloe to miss out on
any of the Halloween fun. For her best

friend's sake, Peggy knew what she had to do.

"Here I am!" she barked, bursting out of the wardrobe. She jumped up on to Chloe's lap and licked her cheek. "I'm ready to be a pumpkin now!"

Chapter Eight

"Peggy!" cried Chloe, cuddling her close. "What were you doing in the wardrobe?"

I was hiding, thought Peggy. *But now I'm going to be brave. I want to be a pumpkin!*

Dad checked the time on Chloe's alarm clock. "Hurry up and get Peggy into her costume. We don't want to be late."

Chloe quickly dressed Peggy in the pumpkin costume. Then she stuck something on her head.

"You look so cute!" said Chloe, holding Peggy up to the mirror. A little hat like a green stem was perched on top of her wrinkly head. The orange pumpkin outfit was softly padded, and around her neck there was a collar of green felt leaves.

Peggy felt a bit silly, but if it made Chloe happy, it was worth it.

"Let's go!" Finn hollered up the stairs.

Downstairs, Ruby was charging

around on her broomstick, shouting,
"Trick or treat! Smell my feet! Give me
something good to eat!"

As they set off down the street, Tiger
was stretched out lazily on his front
porch, basking in the late afternoon sun.
"Nice knowing you, Pig Tail," he called
out to Peggy. "Come back and visit
when you're a toad."

Peggy ignored him, but she shot a worried glance at the sky, looking out for witches on their broomsticks. Hopefully they'd see Ruby with her, and think a witch had already caught her!

On the way to the café, Peggy noticed that many of the houses had jack-o'-lanterns glowing on their porches or in their front windows. When they arrived at Pups and Cups, a vampire in a long black cape greeted them at the door. She grinned, revealing sharp fangs, and said, "Enter if you dare!"

This time Peggy wasn't fooled by the costume. She could tell from the vampire's smell it was just Mum.

Pups and Cups looked amazing, with the ghosts and spiders the girls had made dangling from the ceiling. The tables had been pushed out of the way to make space for guests, and the counter was spread with Mum's pumpkin biscuits, a bowl of fruit punch with gummy worms floating in it, and other Halloween-themed treats. The lights had been dimmed, spooky music was playing softly, and jack-o'-lanterns were flickering in the front window.

Soon, the guests started to arrive. Finn's bandmates came together, and busied themselves setting up their instruments in a corner of the café. Next, Ellie and

Hannah arrived with Princess.

"Happy Halloween!" said Ellie, who was wearing a rainbow-coloured curly wig and a red nose. Her clown costume had big buttons, stripy trousers and a ruffled collar.

"I thought you were going to be a vampire," said Chloe.

"I changed my mind," said Ellie. "Clowns are much scarier than vampires!"

Hannah and Princess were dressed as demon cheerleaders, with matching ra-ra skirts and sparkly devil horns. Hannah, who had also painted her face with scary make-up, shook her red and black pom-poms. "Yay! This is so exciting."

"Nice costume," barked Princess, looking Peggy up and down.

"Now I know how you feel all of the time," said Peggy. The costume was a bit itchy but she couldn't scratch her side while wearing it.

"Ooh – treats!" said Princess, spotting a bowl of dog biscuits and dashing over to it.

Pets and their owners continued to arrive. A lady and her bulldog came as punk rockers. Dotty the Dalmatian came, with her owner dressed as Cruella de Vil. Lola the dachshund arrived wearing a hot dog costume.

"Not very original, I know," she told Peggy apologetically.

After everyone had chatted and eaten some food, it was time to play games. First, the guests took turns bobbing for apples, dunking their heads in a big basin of water and trying to pick up an apple with their teeth.

Ruby went first, and everyone cheered as she pulled her head out of the water, an apple clenched in her mouth.

"Humans are so weird," said Princess, shaking her head. "I just don't get it. I mean – apples? Really? When they could be bobbing for sausages instead?"

After a round of pin the tail on the witch's cat, they played the mummy game – with teams racing to wrap someone up in toilet paper. Chloe

and Ellie won and each got a bag of chocolate eyeballs for a prize. Then Finn blindfolded guests and invited them into his "house of horrors" behind the counter, where they could touch monster eyeballs, ghoul guts and zombie brains.

"It's just grapes, jelly and spaghetti," Peggy whispered to Princess, as they listened to the children squeal.

When the games were over, Mum tapped a spoon against a glass and everyone quieted down. "Thank you all for coming to our very first pug-o-ween party," she said. "I'd like to introduce my son's band, who are going to play a few songs for us."

Finn tapped his drumsticks together in the air and called out, "We are Zombie Disco! And a one, and a two and a—" The band launched into a noisy rock song. Jasmine, wearing her skeleton costume, sang along as she played the keyboard. Zack's arms stuck out of his ghost costume so he could play a wailing guitar solo.

Everyone danced around the café and joined in with the chorus: "*Oooooo, I want to give you a fright! On Halloween night!*"

"I love your brother's band!" Hannah shouted over the music.

"Yeah, they're actually pretty good," said Chloe.

Peggy and the other dogs howled along with the music, too. But Peggy suddenly broke off as the café door opened and a girl with curly hair and glasses came in with a big, shaggy, white dog.

It was the ghost dog!

Peggy froze in horror, waiting for the ghost dog to attack, but to her surprise he hung back behind his owner.

Chloe went over to the girl, who was wearing a bat costume.

"Be careful!" Peggy warned her.

"Hi," Chloe said, as Finn's band finished their song. "I'm Chloe and this is my mum's café. I think I recognise you from the playground. Welcome to our pug-o-ween party."

"Hi," said the girl. "I'm Lily. We live in the big house that backs on to the park. It's a mess, but my parents are fixing it up." The white dog hid behind her legs. "Don't be shy, Albie," she said. "You like it here at the café." She smiled at Chloe. "Your mum invited us to the party because we've been coming here every weekend."

"He's gorgeous," said Chloe, patting the big white dog on the head.

"Albie's having a tough time settling into our new house," said Lily. "He keeps howling because he misses his doggie friends in our old neighbourhood."

What? Peggy couldn't believe what she was hearing. All that howling was because Albie was *lonely*?

"I saw you in the park," Peggy said to him. "Why did you hide?"

"I got scared," said Albie, hanging his head bashfully. "I was afraid you wouldn't want to play with me."

Albie wasn't a ghost dog – he was just
a scaredy-dog!

"Come and meet my friend, Princess,"
said Peggy. "Next time you see us at the
park, you can play with us."

"Yes," agreed Princess. "The more the
merrier."

Peggy introduced Albie to all the other

dogs. Soon, he was chatting happily with Lola about their favourite dog food.

"Ohh! I love liver and bacon flavour," said Lola, licking her chops.

After Finn's band had played a few more songs, Mum announced, "Now it's time to announce the prize for the scariest costumes." Finn did a drum roll.

"And the winners are . . . Hannah and Princess!"

Hannah squealed and jumped up and down, shaking her pom-poms.

"Good grief," said Princess, rolling her eyes. But she cheered up when she saw that her prize was a chewy toy shaped like a ghost.

When the party was over, it was dark outside.

"Can we go trick-or-treating now?" asked Chloe.

"Of course," said Mum. "But stick together – and just go to the houses of people we know on our street."

"Don't worry," said Chloe. "Peggy will

be with us. She'll keep us safe."

"That's right!" Peggy barked. She would always protect her family. Even if it meant being out in the dark on the spookiest night of the year. She would just have to be brave, like Chloe. And like Finn, who hadn't let being scared of spiders stop him from building his tree house. Even Ruby had overcome her fear of heights to climb up to the tree house. They were all brave!

"Want to come trick-or-treating with us?" Chloe asked Lily.

"Yes, please!" she said.

The children spilled out on to the moonlit street, each clutching a bucket to fill with treats. The pavement teemed with ghouls and ghosts, monsters and witches. But Peggy wasn't scared – not even when they went to the spooky old house near the park.

"Trick or treat!" chorused the children, as Lily's parents opened the door.

"Oh my goodness," they chuckled, offering the children a bowl of sweets.

As the children helped themselves to treats, Peggy peered inside Albie's house. The hallway was being decorated with pretty flowery wallpaper, and she could see a big tartan dog bed in the kitchen. She couldn't believe she'd ever thought it was haunted.

151

They continued down the other side of the street, visiting their friends' houses. Soon, the children's buckets were overflowing with treats.

"I love Halloween!" said Chloe. "We should have a pug-o-ween party every year!"

"Yes!" barked Peggy happily. Because Halloween wasn't so scary after all – not when you were with your friends!

The End

Have you read Peggy the pug's first adventure yet?

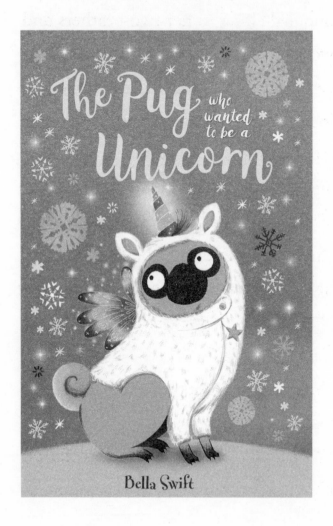

The Pug *who wanted to be a* Unicorn

Bella Swift

Peggy wriggled her little bottom and snuggled closer to her two brothers and two sisters. The five little pug puppies were curled up against their mother's side, snoozing in a furry heap of paws and curly tails. Sighing dreamily, Peggy nuzzled her squashed black nose against her mum's soft, tan-coloured fur.

Suddenly, her mum stood up, nudging the dozing puppies awake with her nose.

"Hey!" yelped Peggy's brother Pablo. "I was sleeping."

Yawning, the puppies clambered to their feet.

"Today's a very important day for all of you," announced their mum, gazing down at the puppies fondly with big brown eyes. "You're going home."

"Aren't we already home?" asked Peggy, puzzled.

"You're twelve weeks old now," her mum said gently. "So your new owners are coming today. They are taking you to your forever homes."

Peggy stared at her mum in confusion, her wrinkled forehead creasing even more. *Forever home? What's that?*

"Don't worry, little ones," the puppies' mum reassured them. "For every dog, there is a perfect owner. I know you will all find yours and be happy in your forever homes."

SLURP! SLURP! SLURP!

A rough pink tongue licked Peggy's face clean.

"Muuuuum!" protested Peggy, trying to squirm away from her mother's sloppy kisses.

"Don't wriggle," said her mother. "I want you to look your best." With one final slurp, she moved on to wash Peggy's sister Polly.

When all the puppies' fur was clean, their mum looked at them proudly. "There! Now you're ready to meet your new owners."

"I hope my owner has a big garden," yipped Peggy's brother Paddy, panting with excitement.

"I hope my owner gives me lots of tasty treats," yapped Pippa, the greediest puppy of the litter.

"I hope my owner likes to take naps," said Pablo, yawning. He stretched out his front paws, sticking his bottom in the air.

"What about you, Peggy?" asked her mum gently. "What type of owner do you want?"

Peggy thought for a moment. A garden would be nice. So would tasty snacks.

But that wasn't what Peggy wanted most of all. At last she said, "I hope my owner loves me."

Peggy's mum gazed at her puppies

tenderly, her eyes shining with affection. "That's what I want for all of you, my dears."

Read **The Pug Who Wanted to Be a Unicorn** to find out what happens next ...

Have you read all these great animal stories by Bella Swift?